CAN YOU DIG IT?

AND OTHER POEMS

UNEARTHED BY
ROBERT WEINSTOCK

FOR MY PARENTS

First Edition

10 9 8 7 6 5 4 3 2 1

F850-6835-5-09350

Printed in Singapore
Reinforced binding

ISBN 978-1-4231-2208-1

Library of Congress Cataloging-in-Publication Data on file.

Visit www.hyperionbooksforchildren.com

POEMS

CAN YOU DIG IT?

Ancient, olden, aged, wrinkled,
Crumpled, tattered, rusted, crinkled,
Buried, hidden, dusty, gritty,
Chipped, cracked, dashed, smashed,
iiiiiiiiiiiiiitty-bitty.
You'll find archaeologists love
What's underground,
Not what's above.

BARTHOLOMEW HUGGINS MCVIGGER

Meet Bartholomew Huggins McVigger.
He's the planet's unluckiest digger,
Digging millions of holes
Twixt the north and south poles—
What a shame not a one was dug bigger.

COPROLITE

My great-aunt was LuAnn Abrue,
The pal-e-on-tol-o-gist who
Was famed for finding fossil poo,
Like giant T. rex number two.
No one discovered more. It's true.

LuAnn avoided ballyhoo;
She sniffed out poop and searched it through
For every hint or tiny clue
(Even at microscopic view)
Of what dinosaurs chose to chew.

Now there were those who pooh-poohed, "Ew...
Old poop is just as gross as new.
I wouldn't wish it on my shoe.
That LuAnn always was cuckoo.
(Her parents both were nut jobs too.)"

But digging in the desert heat,
LuAnn Abrue would oft repeat,
"You are not only what you eat,
You also are what you excrete."

HUGS

I will not hug a dinosaur—
That's one thing that I know for sure.
A giant fossil skeleton
Does not provide much hugging fun.
The idea's lost all its allure—
So I won't do it anymore.

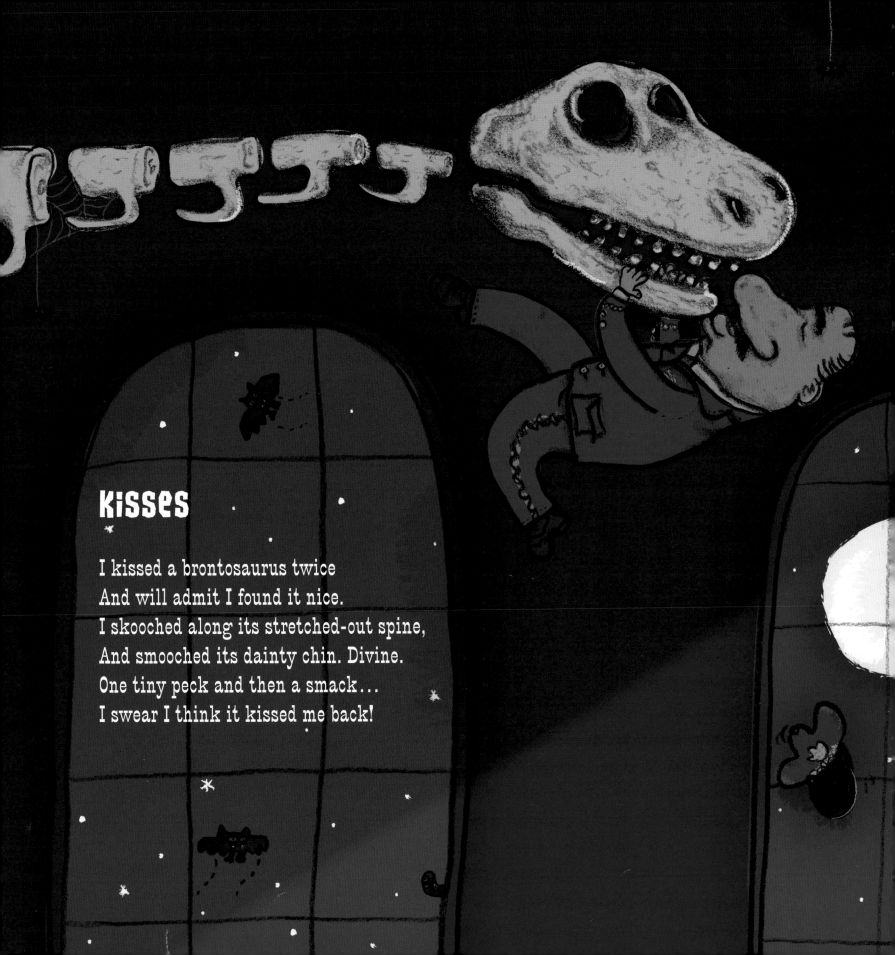

kisses

I kissed a brontosaurus twice
And will admit I found it nice.
I skooched along its stretched-out spine,
And smooched its dainty chin. Divine.
One tiny peck and then a smack...
I swear I think it kissed me back!

GREETINGS

Back in the day before handshakes
  And wet smooches hello,
Cro-Magnon "Hi!"s left painful aches
  And bruises head to toe.

"High five!" was five bonks with a club.
  "Wassup?" was two stone whomps.
"Toodles!" involved a gentle drub.
  "Ta Ta!" entailed foot stomps.

Neighbors would bash their neighbors "Bye!"
  And bite their friends "Good night."
Till some bruised caveman wondered, Why
  Not hug instead of fight?

TUTUS

Cro-Magnon ballerinas were
No dainty twirling prancers.
They stomped and clomped and growled, "Grrrrr!"
Good grief! What dreadful dancers!

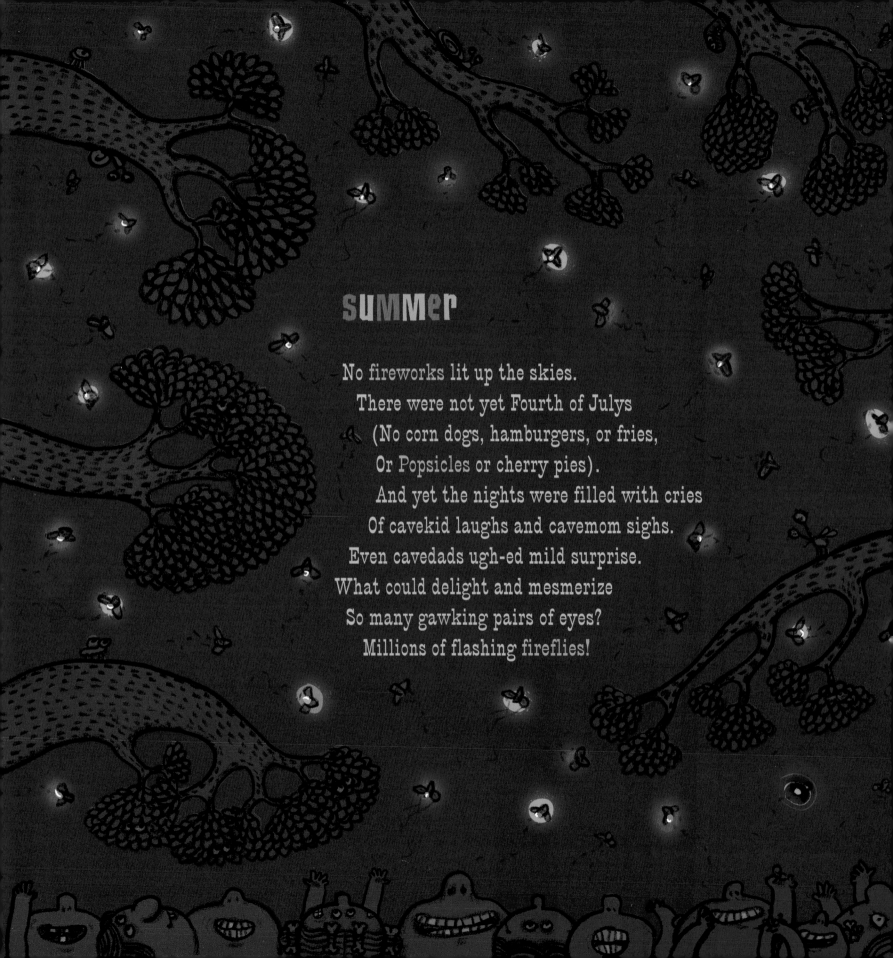

summer

No fireworks lit up the skies.
There were not yet Fourth of Julys
(No corn dogs, hamburgers, or fries,
Or Popsicles or cherry pies).
And yet the nights were filled with cries
Of cavekid laughs and cavemom sighs.
Even cavedads ugh-ed mild surprise.
What could delight and mesmerize
So many gawking pairs of eyes?
Millions of flashing fireflies!

LEFTOVERS

Mom's advice on cooking bison:
Hunt one. Clean it. Rub some spice on.
Exact amounts she's not precise on.
Fix a fire for roasting nice on.
Find a clean stone slab to slice on.
Keeps for weeks if you put ice on.

OLD-FASHIONED

Neanderthals' hats were much worse than their shoes—
Big rocks piled high on your head tend to bruise.
Solid stone footwear was not comfy either.
Most thrifty hominids chose to wear neither.

HISTORY'S BIGGEST DUNCE

Did Neanderthals have homework
That they had to do each night?
And did their parents go berserk:
"Our kid no read no write!"?

Can someone fail arithmetic
If math doesn't exist?
"Class...what am one stone plus one stick?
Carve answer on your schist."

Who hasn't flunked a test just once,
Or failed a dumb pop quiz?
I can't be history's biggest dunce,
But if not me, who is?

TEDDY BONE

No pajamas. No fuzzy bear.
No cozy sheets. It's just not fair!
My blankets itch. My pillow's stone.
I snuggle with a teddy bone.

My bed's a cave—leaky and lumpy.
I'm prehistoric, mean, and grumpy.
Each day I wake up tired and stiff
And cold and ill-behaved. What if

One night I got tucked in like you?
How snug. Next time you whine,
"Boo-Hoooooo!
Nuh-uh! It isn't time for bed!"
I'll happily sleep there instead.

sweet dreams

Poor dinosaur, you cannot sleep?
How about counting tasty sheep?
Yum...One...yum...Two...
Yum...Three...yum...Four...
Sheep leap until you can't eat more.
Full and asleep, you burp and snore.
A finger-licking foolproof cure
For overtired dinosaurs.

BrUNCH

Inside a pterodactyl's nest
Is not the place to be
When chicktyls hatch. Who would have guessed
My omelet might eat me?

BBQ

Brontosaurus burgers are
A drag to barbecue.
They're raw, although their outsides char,
And too darn big to chew.

PREDATOR

Grabbing breakfast by the clawful
Snatching lunch up by the jawful
Wolfing dinner by the mawful—
Makes T. rex-ing seem…well…awful!

Nibbling, gnashing, chomping, breaking
Bones to bits—my stomach's aching.
Gristle? Bleck! I won't partake.
Why can't we stalk some chocolate cake?

T. REX TAG

I didn't mean to eat my friends,
But...Yum...I munched them all.
They came to quite delicious ends—
So tasty, sweet, and small!

I gobbled Fern eight hours ago,
And chomped Earl yesterday.
I can't recall when I ate Flo.
Now no one's left to play.

I never knew a game of tag
Alone would stink this bad.
I'm always "It"! It's such a drag,
I snarfed the friends I had.

SOME FRIEND!

SPOIL-SPORT!

Trajectories

Triple backflips past the peaks of the trees.

Delicate somersaults turned out with ease.

Clasping the swings with the backs of their knees,

Balletic triceratops ride the trapeze.

stegosaurus

I'm unthankfully large and irascibly dense
And a teeny bit prickly and spiny.
I humongously hate being huge. I'm immensely
incensed that I'll never be tiny.

DIPLODOCUS

Trampling, tromping, big tails whomping,
Plodding sauropods are romping.
Long necks threading, short legs treading,
By the riverbeds they're spreading.
Where, one wonders, are they heading?

Waddling, toddling, nostrils whiffing
Snorting, snuffling, treetop-sniffing.
Fern-leaf-chomping, palm-fruit-hewing
Pinecone, seedpod, green-grass chewing.
Crunching, munching, snack-pursuing.
Lunching must be what they're doing.

Sagging bellies, slowly lumbering.
Waking stars too vast for numbering.
Digesting, resting giants slumbering.
Creeping twilight. Full moon beaming.
Sleeping dinosaurs are dreaming.

Earlier

Two hundred fifty million years
  Ago the world is birdless:
    No nightingales or chanticleers.
      The skies are warm and wordless.

    The world is lush with woodland green
  And dressed in ferns and fronds.
  But not a flower can be seen
    About its lakes and ponds.

      No whiskers nose about the ground
        No paws scratch in the brush.
          Just insects click and clack around
            Or hum amidst the hush.

      A spider calmly spins her web—
    So many million years
      Must pass. Millennia will ebb
        Before T. rex appears.